Hugging Hour!

Aileen Leijten

Philomel Books

For my husband, John Rocco,

with all my heart.

PHILOMEL BOOKS

A division of Penguin Young Readers Group.

Published by The Penguin Group.

Penguin Group (USA) Inc., 375 Hudson Street, New York, NY 10014, U.S.A.

Penguin Group (Canada), 90 Eglinton Avenue East, Suite 700, Toronto, Ontario M4P 2Y3, Canada

(a division of Pearson Penguin Canada Inc.).

Penguin Books Ltd, 80 Strand, London WC2R 0RL, England.

Penguin Ireland, 25 St. Stephen's Green, Dublin 2, Ireland (a division of Penguin Books Ltd).

Penguin Group (Australia), 250 Camberwell Road, Camberwell, Victoria 3124, Australia

(a division of Pearson Australia Group Pty Ltd).

Penguin Books India Pvt Ltd, 11 Community Centre, Panchsheel Park, New Delhi - 110 017, India.

Penguin Group (NZ), 67 Apollo Drive, Rosedale, North Shore 0632, New Zealand

(a division of Pearson New Zealand Ltd.).

Penguin Books (South Africa) (Pty) Ltd, 24 Sturdee Avenue, Rosebank, Johannesburg 2196, South Africa.

Penguin Books Ltd, Registered Offices: 80 Strand, London WC2R 0RL, England.

Published simultaneously in Canada. Manufactured in China by South China Printing Co. Ltd.

Design by Marikka Tamura. Text set in Bar May Medium.

The artwork is rendered in watercolor and color pencil.

Library of Congress Cataloging-in-Publication Data

Leijten, Aileen. Hugging hour! / Aileen Leijten. p. cm.

Summary: Drew, who prefers to be called Drool, worries her parents are

never coming back when she spends the night with her grandmother.

[1. Separation anxiety—Fiction. 2. Sleepovers—Fiction. 3. Grandmothers—Fiction.] I. Title.

PZ7.L5345Hu 2009 [E]—dc22 2008027864

ISBN 978-0-399-24680-7

1 3 5 7 9 10 8 6 4 2

To Drool, it felt like her parents had been gone for an awfully long time.

"If you need me, I'll be in the kitchen, Drew," Grandma said.

"It's DROOL, Grandma, not Drew!" Drool said.

Kip was Grandma's house chicken.
He had taken to following Drool around,
everywhere she went.

"Why did Mommy and Daddy leave
me here?" Drool asked Kip.

Kip said nothing.

"Maybe they don't want me anymore,"
she said sadly. "I am an orphan, Kip!"

Drool loved her grandma, but she missed her mom and dad.

"Do you know what time it is, dearie?" Grandma asked. Drool shook her head.

"It's three o'clock, and that means it's hugging hour!"

Grandma and Drool hugged for one whole hour.

Delicious smells curled into Drool's nose.

"What are you making for dinner, Grandma?"
Drool asked.

"First we'll have fried ice cream, then a marzipan
shortcake, then we'll have some porky-pine chocolate
truffles, and for dessert there are Belgian waffles.
But if you don't like that, we can always have oxtail
soup with brain sauce."

"No, no, I like that a lot," Drool said quickly.

Drool threw her leftover
marzipan cake at the ceiling.
  "This is what orphans do,"
Drool whispered to Kip.

Kip said nothing.

After dinner, the piece of cake dropped suddenly into Grandma's lap.

"Look at that, a surprise dessert! I am so lucky that you are here," Grandma said to Drool. Then she went back to her knitting. She was knitting the longest sock ever.

"Why are you making such a long sock, Grandma?"
Drool asked. "No one has legs *that* long!"

"So that there will be plenty of space for goodies
in my sock at Christmas," Grandma answered.
"Would you like me to make you a special sock too?"

"Oh, could you, Grandma? You are so smart!"
Drool said.

Grandma was very smart indeed. She knew
everything, but she had forgotten even more.

"I'll start your sock tonight, but first let's read
a book together."

They made space for Kip on the sofa.

"Grandma, why do you open only one eye?"
Drool asked.

"To let the other one rest," Grandma said.
"Tomorrow I'll use my other eye and let this one rest."

"Really?" Drool was impressed. "Can I try that too?"

"Sure," Grandma said. "But don't forget to open
at least one eye, or else you'll see nothing at all."

Drool was having trouble keeping her eyes open
anyway. It was bedtime.

"I wish Mommy and Daddy hadn't left me,"
Drool said to Kip. "I miss my own bed."

Kip said nothing, as usual. He slept standing
on one foot.

The next morning, Drool woke up to the smell of
Grandma's double caramel pancakes. She made polka
dots on the table with her caramel drippings.

"Look, Kip, just like my dress."

"Grandma, do you want to play dress-up with me and Kip?"

"You go ahead, dearie," Grandma answered. "I've got to work on your sock."

Grandma's dressing room was overflowing with many
years of colorful clothes.

Drool dressed up like Kip and Kip dressed up like Drool.

"Act like me, Kip!" Drool said. "You are an abandoned
orphan now." But Kip persistently acted like a chicken.
He kept jumping out of the dress.

"Let's play hide-and-seek!" she shouted, accidentally spilling lemonade on Kip.

Kip protested loudly and ran away.

"Okay, you're it!" Drool closed her eyes. "Ten-nine-eight-seven-six-five-four-three-two-ONE! Ready or not, here I come!" She sneaked through the hallway, and slunk around the corner, but Kip was nowhere to be found.

"Kip!" she called. "Kiiiipp!" But Kip didn't answer.

"Maybe he has disappeared, just like Mommy and Daddy," she said, her eyes filling up with tears.

Suddenly Grandma appeared, apron in hand. "Is that silly chicken on the loose again?" she asked. "He sure is a stubborn one. What do you say you help me bake triple-decker cupcakes, dearie?" Grandma asked.

Drool loved cupcakes, especially Grandma's triple-decker ones. She helped mix the batter, pour the dough and whip the icing. She sprinkled many sprinkles all over the cupcakes. She even licked the spoon when they were done!

SPRINKLES

DING-DONG sounded the doorbell.

"Can you get the door, dearie?
My hands are full."

Drool was afraid to open the door.

"You want me to open the door all
by myself, Grandma?"

"Don't worry, I'm right here."

Drool was just big enough to reach the doorknob.

"Mommy! Daddy!"

"How was your first sleepover at Grandma's, sweetheart?" Mommy asked.

"I thought you weren't coming back!" Drool said.

"And leave our little Drool?" said her daddy. "Never!"

Drool waved good-bye.

"Can I go back to Grandma's next weekend?" Drool asked.

She already missed Grandma and Kip.